Hurricane!

by Barbara Lieff Fierman

Houghton Mifflin Harcourt™

PHOTOGRAPHY CREDITS: COVER (bg) ©National Oceanic and Atmospheric Administration (NOAA); 3 (bg) ©Lieut. Commander Mark Moran/NOAA Corps, NMAO/AOC; 7 (b) ©EPA/Skip Bolen/Alamy Images; 9 (b) ©National Oceanic and Atmospheric Administration (NOAA); 12 (r) ©Getty Images; 13 (t) ©National Oceanic and Atmospheric Administration (NOAA)

Printed in the U.S.A.

ISBN: 978-0-544-07330-2

13 14 15 16 17 18 19 20   1083   20 19 18

4500710511   B C D E F G

Contents

Vocabulary

weather

air pressure

humidity

water cycle

Stretch Vocabulary

cyclone

swell

surge

eye

dropsonde

Introduction

Hurricane crashes into Gulf Coast!
New Orleans hit hard, Mississippi feels full force!
Massive flooding, 1 million people lose power!

Headlines such as these appeared in newspapers across the United States in August 2005. They highlighted the force of Hurricane Katrina.

Katrina was one of the most powerful hurricanes ever to hit the United States. The storm formed in the Atlantic Ocean and traveled along a path into the Gulf of Mexico. It first made landfall in south Florida on August 25, 2005. When the storm reached the Gulf, its strongest winds were an incredible 200 kilometers per hour (km/h), or 125 miles per hour (mph). Katrina's winds and heavy rainfall caused widespread destruction in Louisiana, Mississippi, and Alabama.

Katrina's floodwaters in New Orleans

Hurricanes—Powerful Storms!

The descriptions of Hurricane Katrina show the power of hurricanes. But what is a hurricane? *Hurricane* is the name for a kind of cyclone. A cyclone is a very large, powerful, and damaging storm with extremely high winds. A hurricane forms over ocean waters in an area of low pressure. The water temperature must be very warm—at least 26.5 °Celsius (80 °Fahrenheit) at the surface. Warm waters provide the energy that hurricanes need to develop, move, and grow in intensity.

Weather conditions have to be just right for a hurricane to develop. Warm air temperature, low air pressure, and high humidity form the perfect setting for a hurricane. And, of course, there's the wind! When winds of at least 119 km/h (74 mph) continue for a period of time, a storm is classified as a hurricane. The winds of a hurricane twist around and around.

Less powerful storms are called tropical depressions and tropical storms. A tropical depression has sustained, or continuous, wind speeds of 61 km/h (38 mph) or less. A tropical storm has sustained wind speeds of 62.8–117 km/h (39–73 mph).

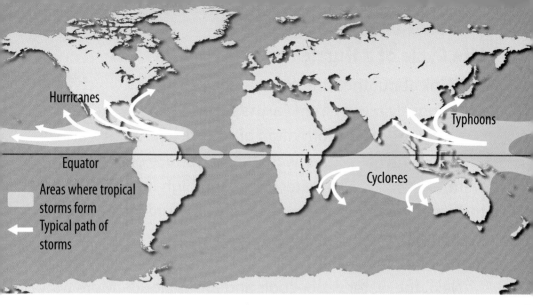

Hurricanes

Typhoons

Equator

Cyclones

Areas where tropical storms form

Typical path of storms

In addition to the damaging winds, hurricanes bring heavy rainfall. Most hurricanes can produce 15–30 centimeters (6–12 inches) of rainfall. The heavy rainfall, in combination with high tides, can cause swells of water along the coast. These swells are known as storm surges. Surges can be as high as 6 meters (m), or 20 feet (ft) and can spread out for 161 kilometers (100 miles). Hurricane Andrew, in 1992, produced a storm surge of 5.2 m (17 ft) at landfall in Florida. A surge like that causes massive flooding along a coast.

Life Cycle of a Hurricane

Think about the water cycle—the process by which water continuously moves from Earth's surface into the atmosphere and back again. The formation of a hurricane is very similar. When a hurricane forms, water at the surface of the ocean warms. This results in water vapor and high humidity. As the water vapor rises, an area of low pressure forms below it. Then, air with higher pressure pushes in below and forms more warm, moist air.

Next, the water vapor cools and forms clouds. More water evaporates and forms even more clouds. Winds cause the system of clouds to begin spinning. As the cloud system spins faster and faster, the eye of the hurricane forms in the center. Believe it or not, the eye is actually the calmest part of the storm. The area surrounding the eye is called the eyewall. This is where the most powerful activity of the hurricane takes place.

A hurricane's winds spin around, pushing water into a mass around the eye. This mass of water, or storm surge, can cause flooding when it hits land. When this storm surge happens at the same time as a high tide, it is called a storm tide. When the tide is high, the flooding is especially severe.

Today, scientists can use computers to predict how great the storm surge will be in a coastal area. Computers gather details about the hurricane's path and strength, the depth of the ocean, and the shape of the land. All these factors are combined to determine the potential strength of a storm surge.

Because hurricanes need warm air and warm water to form, they usually develop at around the same time each year. The hurricane season in the Atlantic Ocean is June 1 to November 30. In the Pacific, it is May 15 to November 30.

In September, 2012, Hurricane Isaac caused a storm surge of more than 3 m (10 ft) on the coast of New Orleans.

Predicting Hurricanes in the Past

Try to imagine this scene: It is morning, the skies are blue, and the sun is shining. Without warning, the sky suddenly darkens, and a steady breeze picks up. In no time, the breeze becomes a powerful wind. Drenching rain falls. Storm surges crash onto the coast. It's a hurricane!

In the past, hurricanes made surprise attacks like this. Scientists didn't have the tools to predict hurricanes. They only received reports about stormy weather from ships' communication systems. Their information about conditions on the ocean was very limited. As a result, people had little time, if any, to prepare for a hurricane.

The National Oceanic Atmospheric Administration (NOAA) has a list of the worst hurricanes to strike the United States. Most of them happened before scientists were able to predict these storms. For example, in 1900, the Galveston (Texas) hurricane caused more than 5,000 deaths. In 1928, the Lake Okeechobee (Florida) hurricane caused at least 2,500 deaths. The New England hurricane of 1938 hit New York and New England with about four hours' warning. About 600 people died as a result of that storm.

Predicting Hurricanes Today

Today, meteorologists have a better understanding of hurricanes and how they develop, grow, and move. They have tools for gathering information on land, over the oceans, and even in space.

For example, scientists use weather buoys in oceans and weather satellites in space to gather weather data. Buoys record data about air, water, surf, and wind conditions. Satellites gather information about cloud cover and track large storms, using radio signals to transmit the data.

Organizations like NOAA are dedicated to hurricane prediction. In 1954, NOAA scientists began tracking hurricanes. They could only predict a storm one day before it hit land, however. By 2003, scientists were able to make predictions five days in advance of a storm!

Scientists were able to track the movement of Katrina and predict its path in advance.

Measuring, Classifying, and Tracking

The Beaufort Scale of wind speeds was one of the first tools used to measure and describe wind speed. In 1805, Admiral Sir Francis Beaufort of England created the scale. It describes a range of wind speeds from 0 to12. Each number refers to a specific strength of the wind and its effects. According to the scale, a rating of 0 indicates calm seas and calm wind. The highest rating, 12, indicates huge waves and hurricane-force wind.

In 1969, scientists named Saffir and Simpson developed a rating scale for a hurricane's wind speed. The Saffir-Simpson Hurricane Wind Scale rates a hurricane's wind speed on a scale of 1 to 5. While storms with a rating of 1 or 2 can be dangerous, those with a rating of 3 or higher are considered major hurricanes. Scientists use the scale to describe an approaching hurricane. Use of the scale lets people know possible dangers and prepare for them.

The Saffir-Simpson scale is based on sustained wind speed.

Saffir-Simpson Hurricane Wind Scale	
1	119–153 km/h (74–95 mph)
2	154–177 km/h (95–110 mph)
3	178–208 km/h (111–129 mph)
4	209–251 km/h (130–156 mph)
5	252 km/h or greater (157 mph or greater)

The yellow parachute at the top slows down the dropsonde so that it can collect, record, and send information about the storm.

Today, scientists also have many technological tools to track hurricanes. They use computers, satellites, airplanes, and buoys to gather information. The information is sent to NOAA and the National Weather Service. Scientists use the information to create reports about weather and water conditions in an area.

Scientists from NOAA and the U.S. Air Force use aircraft to track a storm. They fly right into a developing storm! Then they drop tube-shaped objects called dropsondes out of the planes. These devices pick up information about temperature, air pressure, humidity, and wind. Computers record the information and send it to the National or Central Pacific Hurricane Center. Scientists use the information to make predictions about the path of the hurricane.

Tools and Technology

In most parts of the United States, people get TV and Internet service through the use of satellites. Satellites have been extremely useful in tracking and predicting hurricanes. The first U.S. weather satellite was launched on April 1, 1960. That satellite, TIROS-1, carried two cameras and two video recorders. Scientists believe that this satellite changed weather forecasting forever. Today, satellites continue to become more advanced.

Satellite images and data help scientists make more accurate forecasts and warn people about approaching storms. For example, satellites can examine clouds. They can also read the temperature at the surface of the ocean and pick up thunderstorm activity. This information is put into computer models for scientists to study.

satellite in orbit

This satellite image show views of Hurricane Andrew as it moved west toward land in 1992.

Scientists use computer models to predict the path and speed of a storm. The newest computer models can help scientists predict the chance of hurricanes developing during a hurricane season. They can even predict the number of each type of storm that is likely to develop. The models help scientists decide if a storm is likely to become a tropical depression, a tropical storm, or a hurricane.

The value of these predictions is enormous. With advance warning, people can prepare for a storm. They can stock up on water, food, batteries, and other necessary supplies. If a powerful hurricane is on the way, people can have time to evacuate, or leave, coastal areas before the storm arrives. Communities can prepare and set up shelters. Firefighters, police, and medical workers can make plans for the work ahead. Life can return to normal more quickly.

What's in a Name?

You may have noticed that hurricanes have names. In fact, they have people's names. Why do hurricanes get names when other types of weather events don't?

Hurricanes are named to make it easier to talk about them over a period of time. (Hurricanes usually last a week or longer.) Also, during hurricane season, there might be more than one hurricane at the same time. The names limit any confusion about which storm is being described. Hurricanes start as tropical storms, and it is actually the tropical storms that are named. Not every tropical storm becomes a hurricane, however.

The name of a hurricane must meet several conditions before it can be considered. One condition is that the name be short and easy to understand when reported on radio and TV.

There are 21 names for every year, and there are 6 years' worth of names. The names are assigned in alphabetical order. Why are there 21 names per year? Because ever since records have been kept, it's been rare to have more than 21 tropical storms in one season.

A name is retired, or never used again, if it was used to name a particularly damaging storm. The names Andrew (1992) and Katrina (2005) have been retired forever.

Make a Hurricane Safety Guide

Families living in coastal communities have to be prepared for hurricanes. Work with a partner to discuss ways families can prepare for a hurricane. Think about what you have learned about hurricanes and their effects. Consider what families need to do to protect family members, pets, and property. Together, make a guide that could be used by these families.

Write an Article

Choose a hurricane that occurred anywhere in the world during your lifetime. Read about the hurricane in order to be able to answer *who, what, when, where,* and *how* questions about it. Use the information to write an article about the hurricane as if it just happened. Include a headline, facts, quotes, and interesting stories in your article.

Glossary

air pressure [AIR PRESH·er] The weight of the atmosphere pressing down on Earth.

cyclone [SY·klohn] An extremely large, powerful, and destructive storm with very high winds that spin around in an area of low pressure.

dropsonde [DRAHP·sahnd] A lightweight weather device with a small parachute that is dropped from a plane and measures tropical storm conditions as it falls to Earth.

eye [EYE] The calm area at the center of a hurricane or large tropical storm.

humidity [hyoo·MID·uh·tee] The amount of water vapor in the air.

surge [SERJ] A series of large waves that cause a rise in water level.

swell [SWEL] A long wave or series of waves that continue to form as a result of a storm.

water cycle [WAWT·er SY·kuhl] The process in which water continuously moves from Earth's surface into the atmosphere and back again.

weather [WETH·er] The condition of the atmosphere at a certain place and time.